Zelda and Ivy
KEEPING secrets

Zelda and Ivy
keeping secrets

Laura McGee Kvasnosky

CANDLEWICK PRESS

TO MOM
1924 - 2008

Copyright © 2009 by Laura McGee Kvasnosky

First edition 2009

Library of Congress Cataloging-in-Publication Data is available.

Library of Congress Catalog Card Number 2008933532

ISBN 978-0-7636-4179-5

10 9 8 7 6 5 4 3 2 1

Printed in China

This book was typeset in Galliard and hand-lettered by the author-illustrator.
The illustrations were done in gouache resist.

Candlewick Press
99 Dover Street
Somerville, Massachusetts 02144

visit us at www.candlewick.com

CONTENTS

Chapter One
Keeping Secrets

Zelda looked down from her perch in
the pine tree and saw the boy next door.
"Eugene," she called. "Come here and I'll
tell you a secret."

"Okay," said Eugene. He headed over.

"You have to promise not to tell Ivy," said
Zelda, "because she can't keep a secret."

"Okay," said Eugene. He started to climb.
"Woozy-weasel promise?"

"Woozy-weasel promise." They touched
the tips of their paws together.

"Here it is," said Zelda. "Your mom is the tooth fairy."

"Really?" said Eugene. "My mom is the tooth fairy?"

"Yes," said Zelda. "And don't tell Ivy."

That afternoon, Ivy and Eugene played

at his house.

"Zelda told me a secret," said Eugene. "But I woozy-weasel promised not to tell."

"That's funny," said Ivy. "Zelda told me a secret, too. She made me promise not to tell, too."

"She said you can't keep a secret," said Eugene.

"Hmm," said Ivy. "That's what she said about you, too."

The subject came up again while they
were digging a hole to China.

"I wonder if Zelda told you the same
secret she told me," said Eugene.

"I bet she did," said Ivy.

"Let's say it at the same time and see," said Eugene.

Ivy dug out another shovelful of dirt.

"Okay," she said. "On three. One, two, three . . ."

"My mom is the tooth fairy," Ivy and
Eugene said together.

"No," said Eugene. "*My* mom is the tooth fairy."

"Maybe they work together," said Ivy. "Everyone loses teeth, you know."

"Yes," said Eugene, "that's probably it."

"But Zelda is right," he added. "We're not good at keeping a secret."

Ivy smiled. "When you think about it, she's not so good at keeping a secret either."

"What if Zelda finds out we told?" Eugene said.

"Let's woozy-weasel promise not to tell her," said Ivy. They touched paws and got back to digging.

"This is getting really deep," said Ivy.

"Yes," said Eugene. "We're probably almost to Hawaii."

"Let's keep it a secret when we get to China," said Ivy.

"Okay," said Eugene. He dumped another shovelful of dirt onto the pile. "Let's only tell Zelda."

Chapter Two
APRIL FOOL

Zelda was still half-asleep when she sat
down next to Ivy at the breakfast table.

"My goodness," said Ivy. "Look at that."

"What?" said Zelda.

"Your ears have turned purple."

"Oh, no!" wailed Zelda. She rushed to a
mirror to look.

"April fool," said Ivy.

"You got me," said Zelda. "But just wait.
The day is not over."

When Ivy was not looking, Zelda poured

confetti into Ivy's umbrella.

But the sun came out before they left for the library. Ivy did not take her umbrella.

"Rats," said Zelda. But she smiled a sneaky smile.

Zelda had packed Ivy's favorite picnic
lunch: a peanut-butter-and-jelly sandwich.

"Just for you," she said, pulling it out of
her backpack.

"Thank you so much!" said Ivy.

Before she ate the sandwich, Ivy lifted the top piece of bread—and removed the cucumbers.

"Double rats," said Zelda. "How did you guess that?"

At bedtime, Zelda snuck her smelly socks under Ivy's pillow. "This will get her for sure," she said to herself.

But Ivy decided to sleep with her head at the other end of the bed that night.

"Rats, rats, rats!" said Zelda. "I can never fool you."

About a week later, it rained again. Zelda
could not find her umbrella.

"I'll take Ivy's," she decided.

24

When she opened Ivy's umbrella, the confetti rained down.

"Aargh!" wailed Zelda. "This is the worst April ever! I am my own April fool!"

Chapter Three
MADAME BUTTERFLY

BAM! The back door slammed open and Zelda strode out.

"Mi-mi-mi-mi-mi," she sang.

Ivy and Eugene popped up from behind the lilac bushes.

"Quiet, Zelda," hissed Eugene. "We're trying to catch a tiger swallowtail."

"I can't be quiet," said Zelda. "I'm singing opera, and opera is loud."

She ran across the lawn and jumped up onto the picnic table.

"Mi-mi-mi-mi-miiiii!" she sang even louder.

A butterfly flew up, just out of reach of Eugene's net. "Rats," he said.

"Rats," said Ivy.

"If you like," said Zelda, "you two can be in my opera."

"We may as well,"
said Eugene. "We can't
catch butterflies while
you're singing."

"Besides," said Ivy,
"I love to sing. What
shall we do?"

"I'll be Cleopatra,"
said Zelda. "You can be
my servants."

Zelda rose to her toes for some high

notes. *"I am Cleopatra, the beautiful Queen*

of the Nile," she sang. Then she sang loudly

about riding her camel in the desert.

Eugene and Ivy joined in.

"La-la-la."

"Mi-mi-mi."

"Wait!" said Zelda. "This is Cleopatra's

solo. Servants are supposed to fan the

queen while she sings her solo."

Eugene and Ivy fanned Zelda with their
butterfly nets.

"That's better," she said.

Zelda sang about dancing in her palace.

"Then a snake appeared," she sang.

She grabbed her chest. *"Oh, no! The snake bit me!"*

Zelda sank to her knees. *"Alas! Alas! Alaaaaas!"* she sang. *"I fear I am dying!"*

She slumped to the ground. Eugene and Ivy kept fanning.

They stood by as Zelda gasped out a few more notes. *"La-la-mi-mi-miiiii."*

At last, she lay completely quiet and still.

A butterfly swooped by.

"I'm playing dead," said Zelda out of the side of her mouth. "Sing your part now. Sing sadly, because you miss Cleopatra."

Eugene and Ivy sang out a few soft, sad *mi-mi-mi*'s and *la-la-la*'s.

The butterfly circled back and landed.

"Hold still," Ivy said to Zelda. "There's a butterfly on your nose."

Eugene lifted his butterfly net slowly, then quickly brought it down on Zelda's head.

"You got it!" said Ivy.

"Almost," said Eugene.

Zelda propped herself up on one elbow as the butterfly fluttered away.

"What an opera!" she said. "Let's all take
a bow."